Chihs

PUPNIKS

THE STORY OF TWO SPACE DOGS

WRITTEN AND ILLUSTRATED BY S. RUTH LUBKA

MARSHALL CAVENDISH   NEW YORK

Thanks to Dr. Bruce T. Draine, Department of Astrophysical Sciences, Princeton University, for evaluating the text and sketches.   Thanks to Igor Olegovich Muraviev for providing translations.   Thanks to Adam and Emmy, the children who inspire me the most.   Photo of Oleg Gazenko courtesy of Novosti (London) © 1960.   Kennedy letter excerpt (first paragraph of original letter deleted, as not relevant) and photo of Kennedy family and dogs courtesy of John F. Kennedy Library, Boston.

LIBRARY OF CONGRESS CATALOGING-IN-PUBLICATION DATA
Lubka, S. Ruth.   Pupniks : the story of two astronaut dogs / written and illustrated by S. Ruth Lubka.   p. cm.   Includes glossary of Russian words. Summary: Presents the story of the two Soviet dogs, Belka and Strelka, who were sent into space in 1960, paving the way for the first Soviet manned flight. ISBN 0-7614-5137-4   1.Dogs—Soviet Union—1960—Juvenile literature. 2. Space flight—Soviet Union—1960—Juvenile literature. [1. Dogs as laboratory animals. 2. Space flight.] I. Title.   SF426.5.L83 2003   629.45'0947—dc21 2002155828

Book design by Michael Nelson   The text of this book is set in Westerveldt. The illustrations were rendered in colored pencil.   Printed in China
First edition
2 4 6 8 10 9 7 5 3 1
www.marshallcavendish.com

SPACE EXPLORATION
MEMORIAL, MOSCOW

In memory of the seven who died on the Columbia
Space Shuttle, February 1, 2003

THE FIREBIRD

A Russian legend tells the story of a magical bird
called the Firebird. The bird's feathers give off
brilliant light and great heat like the sun. If a
prince can capture the Firebird, his dream of
marrying the princess will come true. The quest
is difficult and dangerous, but without difficulty
and danger, there are no heroes.

This book is dedicated to Igor Olegovich, my Russian
prince, and to heroes, human and canine, everywhere.

— *S. Ruth Lubka*

*MONUMENT TO YURI GAGARIN
(FIRST MAN IN SPACE), MOSCOW*

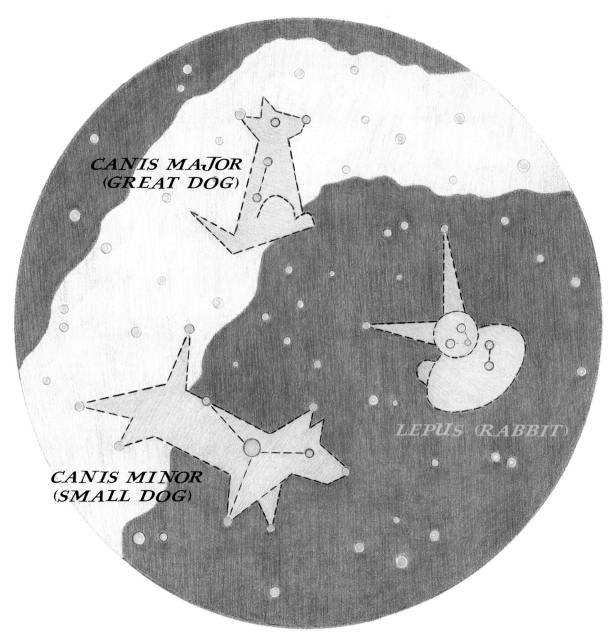

CANIS MAJOR
(GREAT DOG)

CANIS MINOR
(SMALL DOG)

LEPUS (RABBIT)

*L*ong ago, in 1960, two Russian dogs named Belka and Strelka were sent into outer space.

A gray rabbit, forty mice, two rats, one hundred flies, and a garden of flowering plants were sent along with them. As you can imagine, the small spaceship, *Sputnik 5*, was very crowded.

In the time before their space adventure, Belka and Strelka were ordinary pups, but there was something extraordinary about them, too. On the ordinary side of things, they liked to explore street trash and chase rabbits through the snow. They were small dogs with short ears and springy fur. Both were females.

But on the extraordinary side of things, Belka and Strelka were clever strays who could always find a warm, dry place to sleep and enough food to eat, even on a cold Moscow night.

Because they were a good pair, they were chosen for the Russian space program. Scientists named the white pup Belka ("Squirrel"). She was very playful and liked to run.

The other pup was named Strelka ("Little Arrow"). She was younger than Belka. Strelka was mostly white with black ears and a black mask. She was the quieter of the two.

We know little about the rabbit, mice, and rats that would go with the dogs into outer space.

Scientists sent Belka and Strelka into space because they believed that if dogs could make the trip and return safely, people would be able to journey into space, too.

Belka and Strelka went into training near Moscow. Engineers measured them for space suits designed for dogs. The suits helped the pups prepare for space travel.

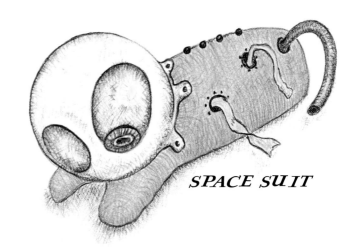

SPACE SUIT

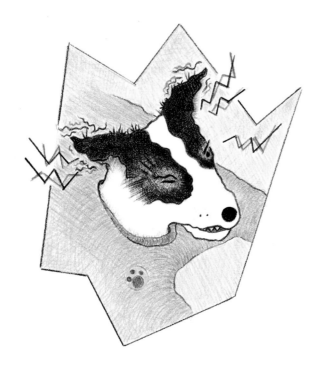

The dogs would have no weight in space. Trainers prepared them to float in zero gravity. The dogs had to get used to loud noises and the shaking of the rocket, too.

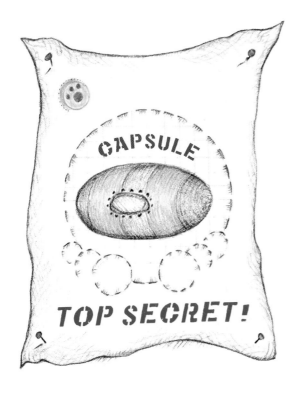

Sputnik 5 carried a capsule to hold the dogs. It was about 5 feet long and 2 feet wide. Belka and Strelka would live inside the capsule, separated by a glass wall. The small dogs had just enough room to lie down, stand, and move forward to eat.

Feeding the dogs in space was a problem. Because of zero gravity, regular dog food would float around their heads. Veterinarians came up with an answer. They invented a healthy space jelly that stuck to the sides of a feeding box. The veterinarians trained Belka and Strelka to slurp the jelly when the cover of the box popped open.

Toward the end of Belka and Strelka's training, photographers came to take pictures of the pups for future Russian stamps. At last the two dogs were ready for their journey.

On the night of August 19, 1960, Belka, Strelka, and their crew of little plants and animals blasted off from Baikonur Cosmodrome, far away from Moscow. Their mission was a secret.

SPUTNIK 5
INSIDE VOSTOK
ROCKET

THREE, TWO, ONE, LIFTOFF!

The rocket twisted around and around as it rose into the sky through big clouds of white smoke. Higher and higher, the rocket carried *Sputnik 5* into outer space.

Inside, Belka and Strelka were pushed and pulled, squashed and stretched. Their eyeballs jammed against their skulls. Their noses twitched.

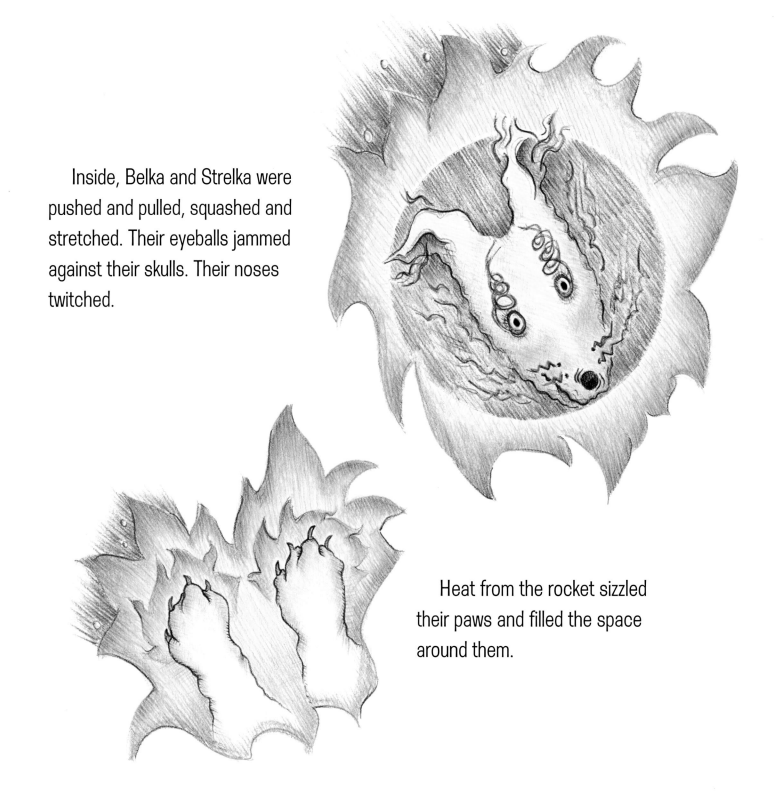

Heat from the rocket sizzled their paws and filled the space around them.

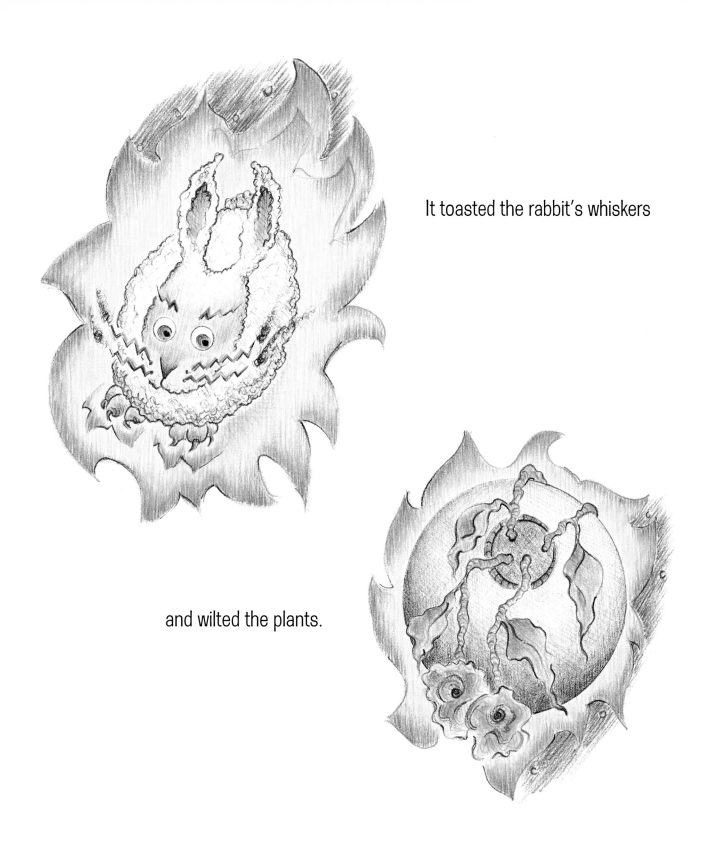

It toasted the rabbit's whiskers

and wilted the plants.

After so much excitement, Belka and Strelka fell into a deep sleep.

Electrodes attached to the dogs recorded their heartbeat and pulse. At first the dogs panted heavily, but after a while, their panting slowed to almost normal. Once in orbit around Earth, Belka began to move. Strelka lay quietly during most of the journey.

STRELKA

BELKA

Back on Earth, scientists studied the data and watched Belka and Strelka on *Sputnik* TV. Because their fur was white, the dogs showed up clearly on black-and-white TV.

The scientists could hear Belka barking into her microphone.

Belka and Strelka did their usual dog business in space. They ate. They slept. But they hated the way their paws hovered weightlessly above the floor. Belka ate too much space jelly and threw up.

SPUTNIK 5

After a day, *Sputnik 5* had orbited Earth
seventeen times. Belka and Strelka sensed
that something was about to change, the
way, for example, dogs know when their
owner is coming home. Heat filled the
space capsule again.

Sputnik 5 plunged through the atmosphere on its way back to Earth. Suddenly, the inner capsule containing the dogs and other animals was ejected from the main spaceship. The capsule had its own parachute and gently floated down through the clouds.

We can only imagine what Belka and Strelka were thinking as they watched the view through the window.

Just in case the capsule did not land where it was supposed to, there were instructions written on the outside of the capsule. They warned anyone finding it:

ВНИМАНИЕ!
ATTENTION!
IF YOU FIND
THIS CAPSULE,
DO NOT OPEN IT!
IMMEDIATELY CONTACT
YOUR LOCAL TOWN HALL!

The capsule landed only six miles from the right place. There was a hard bump as it hit the ground.

Farmers working in a nearby field watched in amazement. They approached the capsule very carefully and studied the instructions. The farmers peeked through the capsule's window. Belka and Strelka stared back from inside. Although the dogs were very tired, they barked and barked.

Before long veterinarians and soldiers in helicopters arrived on the scene. The rescuers opened the capsule, and two happy space travelers jumped out.

Strelka licked everyone in sight. Belka dashed around the field.

The rest of the crew was recovered safe and sound, too.

Moscow Zhournal
21 August 1960
DOGS RETURN FROM SPACE!

The journey into space and back, which had lasted just a little longer than one day, was a great success. Scientists learned important information about what it was like for living creatures in space. As for Belka and Strelka, they were happy to be home.

But this is not quite the end of the story. A few months after her return to Earth, Strelka had six healthy puppies. Russia gave one of the puppies, Pushinka ("Fluffy"), to the president of the United States, John F. Kennedy, and his wife, Jacqueline Kennedy.

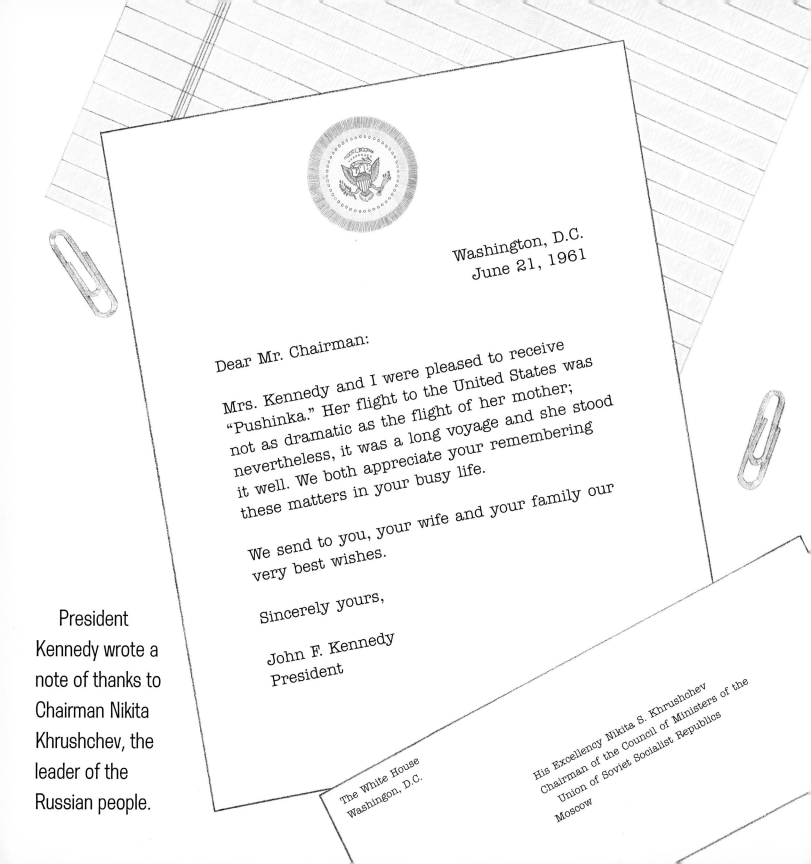

Washington, D.C.
June 21, 1961

Dear Mr. Chairman:

Mrs. Kennedy and I were pleased to receive "Pushinka." Her flight to the United States was not as dramatic as the flight of her mother; nevertheless, it was a long voyage and she stood it well. We both appreciate your remembering these matters in your busy life.

We send to you, your wife and your family our very best wishes.

Sincerely yours,

John F. Kennedy
President

President Kennedy wrote a note of thanks to Chairman Nikita Khrushchev, the leader of the Russian people.

The White House
Washington, D.C.

His Excellency Nikita S. Khrushchev
Chairman of the Council of Ministers of the
Union of Soviet Socialist Republics
Moscow

In time Pushinka had four puppies. Their proud father, Charlie, was one of the First Family's many dogs. Caroline and John John, the First Children, were often seen at the White House playing with the pups. The president liked to call the dogs "the pupniks."

CHARLIE AND PUSHINKA WITH BUTTERFLY, WHITE TIPS, STREAKER, AND BLACKIE

ABOUT THIS STORY

This is a true story, based on facts and imagination, too. Because Belka and Strelka could not tell us how it felt to be in space, I had to imagine that part.

When Strelka's puppy Pushinka arrived in the United States, government officials were worried she might be a spy puppy. Secret Service agents x-rayed little Pushinka to make sure she was not hiding any secret microphones or cameras. She was not.

Mrs. Jacqueline Kennedy kept two of the pupniks for the First Children. She chose two children, one in New York and one in Missouri, to receive the other pupniks.

Russia was called the USSR during the time of *Sputnik 5*. The USSR and the United States were in a race to explore space. Belka and Strelka were the first living beings to orbit Earth and return safely. The information Russian scientists learned from their journey helped to make it possible for a Russian man, Yuri Gagarin, to go into space in 1961.

Russia is no longer called the USSR. It is called the Russian Federation and is working with the United States to explore space.

OTHER SPACE ANIMALS

Dogs, monkeys, chimps, mice, and insects were among the many early animals to go into space.

Some animal lovers have objected to the conditions under which these animals traveled. But most scientists say that animal astronauts were important pioneers that paved the way for human space exploration. Here are a few of the most famous animal travelers:

USA: Sam, a monkey (1959); Ham and Enos, chimps (1961)

Russia (USSR): In 1957 Laika ("Barker"), a dog, was the first creature to orbit Earth. Zvezdochka ("Little Star") was the last dog to go into space before a human made the journey in 1961. Her traveling companion, Ivan Ivanovich, was a dummy that looked like a man. His job was to test human space suits and the ejection seat.

HAM IN SPACE (1961)

BELKA AND STRELKA WITH SCIENTIST OLEG GAZENKO

FROM TOP LEFT: PRESIDENT KENNEDY, JOHN JOHN AND MRS. KENNEDY
WITH PUPNIKS, CLIPPER (STANDING ON RIGHT), CAROLINE WITH
CHARLIE (AT RIGHT), AND SHANNON (BEHIND HER)

GLOSSARY OF RUSSIAN WORDS

RUSSIAN	SOUNDS LIKE	ENGLISH
Белка	Belka	Little Squirrel
Внимание!	Vneemanyeh!	Attention!
Желе	Zhelé	Jelly
Журнал	Zhournal	Journal
Кто?	Kto?	Who?
Спутник	Sputnik	Sputnik
СССР	SSSR	USSR
Стрелка	Strelka	Little Arrow
Что?	Shto?	What?